I0616458

Contents

لَّآ إِلَـٰهَ إِلَّآ أَنتَ سُبْحَـٰنَكَ إِنِّى كُنتُ مِنَ ٱلظَّـٰلِمِينَ

"There is no deity except You; exalted are You. Indeed, I have been of the wrongdoers."

I draw from the well,

dug by a wandering Aramean,

furnished by a prince of Egypt,

clarified by a lowly carpenter,

and irrigated by a desert merchant.

A Father's Wisdom

A father once told his children, "I will give my wisdom to one of you tonight. Pray, and one of you will receive it."

The children left their father's presence and talked amongst themselves. Nearly all of them spoke to each other on how deserving each was to receive their father's wisdom. Later that night, they all prayed.

The next day, their father returned and gestured to one of the children, "This child of mine is the one who will receive it."

The other children were shocked. "He was the only one amongst us who said he was the least deserving!"

Their father replied, "Because this child said he deserved it least, he became the most deserving."

"How?" they asked.

He replied, "His humbleness will keep him from forgetting what you all forgot the moment you left my presence."

"What was that?" they asked.

Their father paused before he answered,

"That the wisdom is mine, not yours."

A Mother's Prayer

A woman came to me with a broken composure, and said, "I miss many of my daily prayers, and I feel I do not deserve to be one of your students, but I wish to be."

I looked at her quietly for a short while and then said,

"Because you said you don't deserve to be, you have become more deserving than most. I would be honored to be your teacher, but go first and tend to your child." She stood up in amazement and rushed away.

My students asked, "How did you know she has a child?"

I replied, "The look of a mother when she is anxious for her child is unique among all desires."

They asked, "What of her missed prayers?"

"None were missed. At those times, she washed herself with a special water that no one could have used but her. It falls in both directions, splashes loudly in heaven, but silently on earth. And it makes the prayer for her."

My students were puzzled and later went to meet the woman, asking her, "Our teacher praised you greatly. May we ask you something about your daily life?"

She nodded in slight confusion.

They asked, "How is it you miss your prayers?"

She answered, "Often, at the time of prayer, no one is around to help me. I do everything for my child while in tears for my desire to pray."

At that moment, my students realized the special water was the woman's tears, and they began to cry in amazement. They told her what I said, and she began to cry as well, saying, "I must see the teacher at once!"

When they came toward me, I walked up to her, smiling, and gently wiped the tears from her eyes.

I said, "Praise be to God who leaves not a single drop uncounted, and weighs the quiet vibration of a mother's heart more than loud praises in places of worship."

A Part of Hellfire

The people asked me, "What is hellfire? It is said to be hotter than the fire of this earth!"

I replied, "It is a fire you cannot see with your eyes, and there are many who burn from a part of this hellfire while still on earth."

They yelled, "Where? Tell us so we can stay away from these people!"

I said, "Look around at those who unknowingly hold a part of the hellfire in their hearts. They pick it up in order to burn others, but it does not leave them.

"Rather, it says, 'Why should I leave the one who holds me so close to their heart?' It begins to burn these people from the inside, many until their death."

They asked, "What is this part of hellfire?"

I told them, "It is the feeling of jealousy."

Then they asked, "How can we save ourselves from this?"

I replied, "When this part of hellfire calls to you, do not answer it. It only calls because it sees an opening in your heart and wishes to fill that space."

They then asked, "Where did this opening come from?"

I answered, "Dissatisfaction, from a lack of understanding the value of oneself."

The Script of the Believers

A man once came to me and said, "I know you are a great teacher with much wisdom. There is something I am driven to accomplish."

He went on to explain what it was and then asked, "Do you think I will be able to accomplish it? I don't think I can."

I replied, "It is as you say it is."

He was saddened, and he asked, "There is no wisdom you can give me to accomplish it?"

I replied, "Wait here with me and you will receive the wisdom in a way that is easiest for you to understand."

Sometime later that day, another man who was scheduled to see me came and asked about accomplishing the same thing. However, at the end, he asked, "Do you think I will be able to? I believe I can."

I replied, "It is as you say it is."

He was happy, and the other man said to him, "You are lucky that the teacher prophesied your success!"

I replied, "I haven't prophesied anything, you have both prophesied for yourselves."

Both were confused, so I sat them down and explained, "The first wisdom you need to have to accomplish a thing is to know that you *will* accomplish it, if you truly believe you will.

"But true belief is often misunderstood. True belief is not a fictional longing in which the mind knows it is a fantasy. True belief is an un-taught, intuitive vision, with a compelling reality of oneself in the future that feels like it must happen.

"But many who believe, later stop believing, and they then go on to say that belief is nothing.

"Then there are those who simply want something with limited motivation and call it belief when it is not, and then they go on to say belief is nothing.

"Then there are those who believe, but at some point, they commit actions that are contrary, and that belief is taken from them and kindled in the heart of someone else who is deserving. To the original person, it becomes something they want but no longer believe. They then fail and go on to say that belief is nothing."

The men asked, "Why is it kindled in the heart of someone else? What about free will?"

I smiled, and said, "Because, in God's script to the movie of Creation and its unfolding, all that has to be said, must be said, and all that is supposed to be done, must be done.

"We are given the free will to accept or deny our roles, and the free will to live with good or bad character, but we are not given the choice to write the roles that are laid out in the script.

"And if an actor does not play the role in the script that was designated for them, that actor is eventually replaced with another, but it delays the execution of the movie."

Claims Manifested

My students asked, "Teacher, may you share a part of your prayers with us?"

I replied, "Yes. In the mornings, I pray: Whether they choose to do good or bad, all of mankind testifies to Your name and ways. Yet so few perceive, and even fewer understand. May it be in Your plan that I continue to teach others, and to keep myself learned as well."

They asked, "How do people testify to God's name and ways?"

I told them, "For every claim you make with strong intent, God will test you on it by creating a situation in which you have to prove the truth of your claim. If you cannot live up to it, you are made an example of. If you do live up to the claim and pass the tests, it warrants ownership, meaning that you will then be that which you claimed to be.

"Also know that those who speak in absolutes will be put into a situation where they will have to carry out the absoluteness of their statement. But they will fail and be made an example of if they don't repent from it in due time, so beware not to use this language."

My students asked, "Why does God do this?"

I replied, "Because only God can speak in absolutes and be truthful in them. God speaks, and His words are proven instantly, for God is the active principle itself.

"We, being made in the image of God, have the ability to speak a claim, but we are bound by laws and the parameters of time and physicality; therefore, claims must be justified by actions.

"When spoken, those words are heard by the universe, and the universe responds, 'So and so has made a claim with firm belief; let their claim be proven by action.'

"Subsequently, the person is given a single or several tests to prove their claim. However, in the case of absolutes, the person fails and is made an example of, as a testimony to the only being which is absolute or can produce absolute results: God."

I shook my head in sadness, saying, "How many such testimonies are there in history and around us now, yet so few perceive them.

"So seek to make claims which are not absolutes, claims for things that you are passionate about accomplishing, and then welcome the tests to earn those things with joy, knowing the test would not be sent unless you had the ability to pass and manifest your claim into the physical world.

"And try your best to not be anxious, for anxiety is like the wind from the fast speed of a hand trying to grasp that flower which it calls a wish: the flower flies away. Whereas, when people move their hands calmly and with patience, they grab hold of what they wish for.

"Lastly, keep in mind that moments of anger are themselves part of the test to see whether or not you deserve the changes you wish for. Conquer these moments in silence, and your reward will be announced in the unseen and unheard world. Work hard and be patient while the change manifests from the metaphysical to the physical world."

Consistency

My students asked, "When striving for something, why is it that some people achieve it faster than others, even when they seem to have the same starting point?"

I explained, "When earning something legitimately, your positive future calls forth the sins of your negative past to come to terms with it before it can proceed.

"So, some people are presented sins from their past that would block the thing they're striving for, and they are put in situations in which they must fix those unchecked issues when first starting out on a new path.

"Whereas, people who have already made amends for and fully learned from their past sins before they start, will move more quickly towards their goal.

"Also, you must be determined, but not overly aggressive. If you care about your goal, then let your passion for it be as controlled and consistent as the watering of a plant. Giving it too little water will allow it to die, but giving it too much will destroy both you and the plant."

My students asked, "How can too much cause both to die?"

I told them, "When people become so lost in emotion that they lose sight of who they are, they forget the true purpose of their mission in the first place.

"It becomes like a flood, where both the person and their crop are destroyed and washed away."

Criticism

My students asked, "Teacher, how will we know when criticism from a person is genuine and when it is not?"

I replied, "When you discover that the person also criticizes themselves, then you know their criticism is genuine. But if you find that they never criticize themselves, pay no attention to them, for no person is perfect. Those who clothe themselves in pride lie to themselves and those around them.

"And remember, time is precious. For any issue, first seek those who have the experience, and then among that group, if you find those who openly tell you of their past mistakes, take their words as you would take a precious gem, and hold them close to you.

"And do not judge based on appearances, for the secrets of God are found in those places where you must sacrifice ego in order to receive them. Just as you find diamonds in the darkest coal, and gold in the filtered dust of stones, so does God place value in what looks insignificant on the surface.

"And yet how many people were judged on their surface and thrown away? Indeed, we have lost diamonds. Indeed, we have lost gold."

Destination

My students asked, "What of repentance? Why is it that some see the fulfillment of their repentance in this life, but some do not?"

I replied, "When God created the universe, one of the fundamental laws was that repentance be given to those among creation who have free will. Just as you can recover in the body, so too can you recover in the spirit, with repentance.

"Think of your life as you would a vehicle that is taking you to your destination. The wrong actions steer the vehicle in the wrong direction. If you don't adjust course in a certain amount of time, you will veer too far, to the point where an adjustment in course will *still* not bring you to the destination before your time is up.

"But know this good news: When you die before reaching your desired destination, God looks at the direction you were going before you died, and if it was the right one, He counts you as one who arrived.

"So, constantly seek to repent and bring yourselves back to the right direction, and you will see the fulfillment of your repentance, in this life or the next."

Ego

One day, while I was teaching, someone barged into my classroom and said, "I've heard that you know how to bring peace between people with huge differences amongst them. This is preposterous. How is it that you can make both sides win in an argument?"

I replied, "By causing both of their Egos to lose."

I continued to speak to this person and their friends for hours about ego, and the many ways to squelch it.

After they left, some of my students arrived and saw me in prayer saying, "I am but dust given life, and I am forever thankful. All that I am is from You and will return to You."

As I was repeating this, the students who had just arrived said, "Maybe the Teacher is saying this because he is regretful of something?"

But one who was close to me responded to them,

"The teacher and I were somewhere earlier where the people were honoring and praising him nonstop, so he is not saying this for a mistake; he is saying it to remain humble."

Expelling Negativity

I told my students, "Be quick in expelling negative energy from an insult, since negative energy is a fire that only grows heavier over time and burns its container.

"But be careful, simply expelling it from yourself unto another makes that fire fall back even greater upon you, and spills upon those close to you."

My students asked, "Teacher, how then do we expel negative energy without creating more of it?"

I asked them, "Why does a person in a gym not become angry at their trainer's talk, and at the pain they feel when they exercise intensely?"

They said, "Because they know they'll become stronger for it."

I replied, "Then know that when you are insulted and do not insult back, you are building your patience to help for later trials in life. In this way, you will not harbor the fire that burns within you, but rather you will expel it by using it as a fuel."

I then asked them, "Why is it that when one worker insults another worker without realizing that their boss is behind them, the one who was insulted stays quiet?"

They replied, "The one who was insulted stays quiet because they see the boss and know the boss will punish the one who sent the insult, and they know that if they were to say something retaliatory, they would be punished as well."

I smiled and said, "Yes, and in that way, know that the Creator is always aware. So do not act like one with his back turned."

I went on that day, explaining how to expel negativity in its different forms, using different parables, until all of them understood with the same clarity.

Fear of Freedom

One day, as I was walking with my students, we came across a man in tears.

I asked the man, "Why are you crying?"

He said, "I have lived my life being sure of everything, but I was wrong to do so, and I realize now that I don't know anything."

I told him, "Let these become tears of joy, since you have just broken the chains of slavery, and now you are free."

But the man became upset at this and ran away in anger.

I then said to my students, "This man wishes to be back in the arms of his slave-master."

My students asked, "How is that? And who is his master?"

I replied, "Those who show contempt for humility are attracted by the security of a fixed opinion, regardless of its truthfulness. In that way, they love to be slaves. Their own Ego is their master."

While my students were reflecting on this, I added, "Blessed are you, for I can see you checking the gates of your mind, seeking to find any chains there that may be left unbroken. It is unfortunate that this man has turned down becoming one of the wisest people."

My students asked, "How?"

I replied, "The cup of the mind cannot be filled with wisdom if it does not know it is empty, and the cups that are completely emptied are filled with the most wisdom, as it was with the wise men of the past.

"Remember that the ones who make decisions solely based on the perception of others are slaves who have *put themselves* in chains. They often come to me, wondering about the source of their pain, and I tell them, 'You wish to be yourself, and every time you move in that direction, the shackles of slavery are pulled in your mind.'

"I am from the line of those who break the shackles and help others to do so as well."

Finding Friendship

A man came up to me with a troubled look, and said, "I don't know who my true friends are. How do I solve a situation like this?"

I asked, "Do you wish to have only the truest of friends around you?"

He exclaimed, "Yes! And I would do whatever needs to be done in order to have just that."

I told him, "Put together a party for your friends and announce there that you've lost all your wealth and special connections. Then tell those you spoke badly of at some point that you did, and apologize for that.

"Afterwards, plan for another party. Those who show up to your next party are your truest friends."

The man frowned. "I can't do that," he said.

I then put my hands on both his shoulders and looked into his eyes.

I told him, "You wouldn't like who you are without material wealth and Ego, so how then can you find the truest of friends...if you can't be a true friend to yourself?"

Following

One day, two people were standing nearby while I was teaching. One spoke to the other, saying, "Why must we follow anyone? We can find our own way!"

The other said to him, "You're a fool for taking such risks! I will simply follow whoever is around me at the moment and play it safe."

I said to them, "Ones who refuse to follow anyone will find themselves demanding attention from everyone, and they will bring about their own destruction.

"And ones who follow anyone will find themselves ignored by everyone; they will bring about their own destruction.

"But the ones who take the time to discern amongst the sayings and doings of all people, and who follow only that which they find to be righteous, while sifting out that which is sinful—they will be respected by all."

The two people stormed out upon hearing this, and my students said, "They don't respect us for following this teaching, so how is your teaching true?"

I replied, "They hate outwardly, but this hatred is the outer cover to the inner cover of jealousy. What lies beneath both is the admiration and respect they have for you in their hearts, but they are blind to it.

"And remember, the demonstration of deep perception brings out admiration from those who love you, and fear from those who hate you."

God Is Love

A man once came to me and said, "You teach that God loves but also punishes, and that we must love but also fear Him. But I represent those who only *love* God; we don't believe in a God who punishes. Our understanding of God is far greater than yours!"

I replied, "You were born from the religious folk who use fear and punishment maliciously for control and for their own Egos, those who have lost the understanding of fear and love."

I closed my eyes and continued, "Praise be to God who rightfully puts the ramifications of sin upon the children, but gives children an opportunity to earn the good by restoring the balance."

I then said to the man, "You can never truly love God if you do not fear Him."

The man said, "Prove it!"

I told him of a story:

There was once a King with 2 children who were called

Dallan and Mustaqim. The King loved his children very

much. He told them, "I made a promise when I created this kingdom, that it would operate according to certain laws so it can regulate itself with justice. I vowed that I would never break my own promise, because if I did, it would be an injustice, and that is against who I am. It would undo everything I have built. You, my children, live within this kingdom, not outside of it; always remember that."

As the years went by, Dallan would periodically buy the King gifts and sing beautiful words, saying "I love you the most! You are love itself! You would never wish to hurt me!"

But the King was saddened by Dallan, and Dallan was blind to it.

The king said to himself, "Dallan doesn't care to ask about his sins, let alone correct them. If I were to force him to ask about his sins, that would be an injustice to those who ask in earnest and of their own volition. It is against my nature to commit injustice.

"But I want the best for him, so I will delay judgment for many of his sins, give him credit for whatever good he does now, and put him in situations where he can be useful in the kingdom and still have time to repent. This way, at worst, he will enjoy the time he has now before my final judgement."

Mustaqim, on the other hand, couldn't afford to bring lavish gifts like Dallan, and he couldn't sing praises as beautifully, but every time he would come to speak to his father, he would ask him, "Father, is there anything I have done that bothers you? I admit I have broken some of your laws, and I am embarrassed by this. Perhaps I've broken some of your laws without knowing, I'm not sure. Father, I am fearful of your judgement!"

The king smiled and told Mustaqim, "I have received some reports, but they are always small. I forgive you for whatever wrongs you have done to me between the last time I saw you and now.

"And as far as the others you may have offended, you must fix it with them, or do your best to. Don't let your ego prevent you from doing so, for the day will come when you would regret that. Understand that I may pay you back for many of your sins before the final judgement, but this is because you wish to be close to me; therefore, I wish to be close to you and help to purify you. You may also experience what may look like suffering for a sin, but it is just something to build you for a greater purpose.

"You may also confuse the punishments of those near you with being your sin, when they are not.

"My son, because you continuously inquire, I can open your eyes to these things in justice, without violating my own promise, and it brings me joy."

Many years passed, and finally the Judgement Day that the King ordained for everyone in the kingdom came to pass.

When the time came for Dallan and Mustaqim to come forward, Dallan looked at Mustaqim and said, "You should have spoken of our father's love more often! Our Father is a loving King like no other!"

Then the prosecutors came forward with a long list of violations by Dallan.

They enumerated thousands of people Dallan had hurt, and petty crimes, some of which he knew, and some of which he wasn't aware.

Dallan cried out, "Father, I loved you more than anyone! Your love is greater! Your love is greater!"

The King said to his son, "You bought me gifts and sang

great praises, but you never loved me, for if you did, you

would have cared about my promises, about my justice,

about who I am. You would have been afraid to hurt me,

just as any person is afraid to hurt the one they love."

The prosecutors then grabbed Dallan and dragged him

away.

Mustaqim stood shaking in fear, and asked, "Where are my

prosecutors?"

The King smiled and said, "My beloved son, all your life

you were afraid of my judgement, afraid to break my

promises, afraid to desecrate my name.

"Therefore, for you today, I am love."

Upon hearing the end of the story, the man walked away with a look of concern on his face.

My students asked, "After hearing that whole story, he was only concerned?"

I told them, "Concern is the opening of the heart."

Glimpse of Heaven

One day, at a social gathering, my students came up to me and asked, "We were discussing which place, among the riches of this world, would give us the best glimpse of Heaven. May you tell us which one of them it is?"

I called upon a small child and lifted him up. The child smiled at us and began to giggle, saying, "Friends!"

I then said, "You know what kind of place a person is from, by their character. This child has just come to this world from the place you speak of and knows no enemy, has no hatred, is full of love, and is in a constant state of wonderment."

I hugged the child and said, "So, here in my arms is among the most valuable of riches in this world: a glimpse of Heaven."

He Wished to Be Good

One of my students came and told me that he finally found a solution to a problem he had for years.

I closed my eyes and smiled. "Ar-Rahman, Al-Hadi [The Merciful One, The Guide]."

My student asked, "I understand why you said Al-Hadi, but why did you mention God's Mercy before His Guidance?"

I answered, "Because God's Mercy does not start with solutions or receiving material things. God's Mercy starts with time—the granting of time itself to make repentance, search for the solutions, and recover from mistakes.

"First is Mercy, then is Guidance."

Afterwards, a man came from afar, running towards me with tears, saying, "I wish to be good! Help me!"

I smiled and said, "You were running, but God in his mercy has outrun you and made you good before you even stepped out of your house to see me."

"How is that possible?" he asked.

I replied, "The moment a person truly wishes to be good, they become good. It is a gift given immediately, but only unwrapped with actions."

This calmed the man, and he looked happy once more.

But I gazed with tears in my eyes upon the sea of people in our vicinity, and said, "Yet how many among mankind are still running, thinking they don't have God's Mercy, and how many gifts wrapped in guidance has God rushed to give that are never unwrapped?"

The One-Eyed

There was once a person who was invited to join different political parties. Each party had aspects this person liked, but there were vagrants in each party that stood out to him.

He asked the leader of one of the parties, "I'd love to join you, but what about these vagrants? It seems you make excuses for them."

The leader responded, "We can't look bad in front of the other parties. They want to discredit us and are looking for any chance to do it, so for the sake of saving our party's pride, we defend the worst of us to protect the best."

The person told the leader, "This logic is flawed and only furthers the divide between all people, causing resentment among the youth for the entire institution. It also furthers the divide between you and what your party originally stood for."

My students heard of this happening, and asked me about it: "Which is correct, the right or the left party?"

I said, "Either alone is incorrect; rather, both are necessary to achieve balance. You must strive to be like the prophets. When they saw people moving too far left, they veered them to the right. When they saw them moving too far right, they veered them to the left.

"Seek to create a home and society in which there is balance. For if someone refutes the viewpoint of the left or the right completely, it is like being blind in one eye. You will lose depth and drive off the straight path into destruction."

Some of my Muslim students were frozen by this. I smiled and told them, "Some of you know that there will be one who will come, blind in one eye, who will lead the world astray. The story of the political parties was to explain to you how the Ego of those in both parties will create the grounds for this man to come and deceive the people."

They asked me, "In which eye will he be blind? The left or the right?"

I told them, "The right, for it is easier to deceive with the left eye. Even then, his will be an exaggerated left eye, set far to the left. And he will have an outwardly attractive, false ease, false love, and perverse guiltlessness.

"The way is being prepared for this great deception day by day. And most do not perceive that those of the far right, who are blind in the left eye, are causing it to happen faster with their heartlessness, prejudice, misogyny, and lack of empathy."

Hired Hands

I taught my students, "Valiant is the searching Agnostic, but deluded is the staunch Atheist: One sits on the branches of the tree of life, saying, 'I do not trust what was told to me because I know the nature of man, so I shall continue to climb down to understand the meaning of this tree and how we came to have the fruit of its branches.'

"While the other sits on the same branches, saying, 'I do not need to climb down any further. This tree exists for no reason, and this fruit is of our own making.'"

My students asked, "What is the fruit?"

I replied, "Morals and Ethics."

"Why has God then allowed the Atheists to be so successful in their cause?" my students asked.

I answered, "Imagine a King who wished to build a house as a model for others to follow. He built it using the sturdiest of foundations that would never fail. He customized the rooms of the house for a select group of people who earned the right to be entrusted to dwell in it. He told those people to teach others to use the same foundation to build their houses.

"After some generations, the descendants of the entrusted ones began to conflate the infallibility of the foundation with the customized rooms of their dwelling, and thus they acted haughtily towards others. Their haughtiness then turned into competition amongst themselves and resulted in baseless hatred.

"So, the King inspired one righteous man among them to teach the difference between the rooms and the foundation, in order to bring love once more into their hearts and save them from exile. However, most of the people ignored this righteous man and his teachings, so the King demolished part of the house and exiled its misguided inhabitants, to protect his name and truth from being further desecrated.

"Some of these exiles—the followers of the righteous man inspired by the King—like children left alone, were adopted by a foreign people, who infused their own ideas upon them, and gradually caused them to separate from the rest of the exiles. The King allowed these adopted ones to flourish and be a harsh reminder to the rest of the exiles to this day.

"From that point on, the knowledge of that impenetrable foundation spread across the world. The King also fulfilled a promise made with another group of people, that he would build them a house on that same robust foundation.

"The King inspired a builder and caused him to succeed, but the generations after that builder failed, just as the entrusted ones had.

"The King had much patience, though. He waited, watched, and reserved judgment, while all the people, with all of their houses, built up their arrogance to a tipping point, due to their constant argument over who has 'the true house.'

"With no room left to exile, the King looked for a people who were not involved, and the only ones left were those whose hearts were completely blind, so the King inspired them to destroy all the houses everywhere.

"They did not recognize the King as the one who ignited their desire, nor did they care of the foundation as anything other than what they could see with their physical eyes. They were hired hands, mercenaries who did not truly know their employer. These are the Atheists."

My students then asked, "What will happen after this?"

I told them, "They will continue to destroy until no house is left unbroken and the children cry out, 'Everything we believed in was false! There is no King!' That is when the one-eyed will appear to take the world into complete deception.

"During this time, there will be one person found washing debris off of the impenetrable foundation, and the righteous few from each house will join him. People will ask, 'What are you doing? Are you seeking to build a new house?'

"They will reply, 'No, but now that the mercenaries have destroyed all the houses, the foundation can be cleansed with ease!'

"The King will look upon these people clearing the debris and say, 'These are a people who saw the homes of their forefathers destroyed before their eyes and did not forget me. They focus not on the idea of whose house was greater, but rather on making sure my foundation is clear to all.'

"Afterwards, the King will separate those people from the arrogant and one-eyed, and a great war will occur in which only the righteous will remain.

"On that day, the impenetrable foundation will be cleared of whatever debris was left. A house of houses shall be built, and all will know the King and live in peace."

Holding onto the Past

Let go of the past, or you will continue to feel pain in your soul even after the other corrections you make in your life.

My students asked, "What is the pain like?"

I replied, "It's like a person in a fast-flowing river who has corrected all those things that would cause a leak in their canoe, but refuses to go where the river wishes to take them. They hold onto the part of the riverbed they anchored onto many years ago, and the river continues to pull them forward."

My students then asked, "What will happen to them?"

I replied, "Relative to how long they continue to hold on, they will feel the pain of being pulled in two different directions. Some let go sooner, while some continue to hold on until the river tears them apart.

"But I implore you to always trust in the river of life. It will take you where you are supposed to go, not always where you *think* you should."

My students asked, "Is there anything we can do to help make the river of life get us to our destination faster?"

I told them, "Be appreciative, because the state of appreciation is a receptive one that draws blessings in, like rushing water that pushes you faster through the river.

"And don't be like those who think the water comes from a limited source; their misunderstanding provokes them to steal from their neighbors when they can. But this only causes a rupture from which the extra water flows through themselves and outward, propelling farther ahead the ones they stole from."

Indecision

I told my students, "The Angels rejoice at one who is in the state of reflection, while Satan cries in anguish. But during this time, there comes a moment when the Angels begin to cry and Satan begins to rejoice."

My students asked, "When is that moment? Can it be avoided?"

I said to them, "It is the moment when Reflection turns into Indecision. Avoid it by taking action."

They replied, "What if our timing is wrong? How will we know?"

I asked, "How do you know when to inhale and when to exhale?"

My students answered, "We feel the need to take in air, so we do, and then we feel the need to exhale, so we do."

I smiled. "In the same way, you will feel when the time is right.

"But now you are far from perfect in discerning the right time, for this crooked world has constantly clouded this feeling from the time of your youth. However, with God's permission, I will teach you how to clear the mist and remember again."

My students said, "Indeed, you are one of the greatest teachers to ever live!"

I replied, "I am not, for in the world to come, small children will teach and remind each other in a way even greater than this."

Language of God

A man asked me, "How should I speak to God? It seems He does not answer me when I speak to Him."

I said, "What do you want to ask Him?"

He said, "I want to ask that I should keep my wealth. What special words should I say?"

I told him, "When you are put in a position where you can show off your wealth to gain others' praise, do not do it. And when you are put in a position where you can genuinely compliment the wealth of others, do so every time."

The man asked, "What does that accomplish?"

I told him, "When you show off your wealth, you tell God its value is purchased by the sight of others, and therefore, He causes their sight to spend it away.

"When you instead promote another's wealth, you tell God the value of wealth is from it belonging to a person, and therefore, He causes your own to remain with you."

The man said, "But these are not words, these are actions?"

I asked him, "When God blessed or punished you, did it come as words or actions?"

"Actions," he said.

I replied, "And what caused those blessings or punishments that came back to you?"

He said, "My actions."

I said, "So, know that you are always speaking to God with your actions, and His reactions are Him speaking to you.

"Therefore, direct the conversation to that which you desire by the language of action, since this is the language of the Creator."

From that day forward, I never saw a man so excited about his daily conversations with God.

Life Plays Back to Us

A stubborn young man came to me and asked, "What hope is there for me? I'm a horrible sinner, and I heard you say that all of our actions will be played back to us in the next life, and that part of the fire of Hell is the unconfronted guilt of our negative actions playing back to us."

"Yes," I said.

"You also said that genuine repentance and correction for those negative actions in this life would save us from that fire."

"Yes."

"So how can it be that a person will be saved from that fire, if even after corrected, they still have to see their negative actions in the next life?"

I smiled. "Tell me of the movies you have seen where a character has done horrible things, but before the movie ends, they repent and seek to correct their actions. Even if they die the moment after they have a genuine intention to correct their wrongs, all of the audience empathizes and praises them, saying, 'They were righteous on the inside all along, and even though they did wicked acts in the past, our perception of all of it has changed.'"

The young man understood and started to cry.

I looked at my students and said, "Alhamdulillah [Praise be to God]; look now and understand the verse where God mentions stones that split, the openings from which water flows forth.

"Behold: a hardened heart has split, and from its eyes water flows forth."

Modesty

Some people came to me and asked, "What about the women who do not cover themselves appropriately; they are not modest. Scorn them!"

I told them of a vision I had: "I saw a modestly-dressed woman, blindfolded, pouring milk into the jug of another woman."

The people asked, "Who were these women? What does it mean?"

I told them, "The blindfolded woman was a modest woman who was verbally abusing another woman for not dressing as she does. The modest woman could not see that her good deeds were pouring into the soul of the woman she scorned."

The people were shocked.

I continued, "I saw another vision. I saw a woman who was dressed in revealing clothing, blindfolded, pouring milk into the jug of another woman."

The people asked, "What does it mean?"

I said, "The revealingly-dressed woman verbally abused the other woman for not dressing as she does; she could not see that her good deeds were pouring into the soul of the woman she scorned."

The people became confused and shouted, "No one is safe! Whether modest or immodest, they're all bound to failure!"

I put up my hand and said, "Yet I have another vision. I see the same two women, the one who was modestly dressed and the one who was revealingly dressed, both with their eyes open, sitting together and laughing, as they drink from an endless river of milk and honey."

The people looked surprised. "How can it be? How can both be in heaven?"

I told them, "There was once a modest woman who did not take false pride in her modesty, and a revealing woman who respected those who dressed modestly. Therefore, neither was blindfolded, and both saw each other one day and had a conversation.

"In doing so, they realized why they both lived the way they did. The modest one chose to no longer be extreme in her modesty, and the revealing one began to dress more modestly.

"Together they will sit and laugh in paradise, drinking from the two deeds that saved them."

The people asked me, "What are those two deeds?"

I replied, "Love and understanding."

My Teacher's Grave

I had a vision of a man furiously throwing dirt at people while standing above the grave of another man.

I asked, "Why are you so angry?"

He replied, "I am defending the grave of my teacher; he was a great man. I throw dirt at those ignoring me, then when they look, I tell people about my teacher, and they say, 'His name is but dirt!' So, I continue to throw dirt at them."

I looked at the grave of his teacher. "I too know of your teacher; he indeed was a great man. But I know why they do not believe the same as we do."

"Oh? Tell me my brother, why?"

I replied, "Turn your sight inward, and look back at his grave."

He looked and began to cry out, "Who has done this? There is dirt on the grave of my teacher! No one can recognize him this way! No wonder they said as they did!"

I told him, "Each time you pulled your hands back to throw dirt at people, more dirt fell on your teacher's grave than what was thrown. And when the people looked, they said, 'His name is but dirt.' And what are these adornments? Our teacher never asked for this."

The man tearfully replied, "I wished to adorn his memory with gold and silver, with grandeur, because I love him."

I said, "You have unintentionally shaped his memory as you would shape your own."

The man, fully realizing his sin, said, "I stood to represent my teacher the most, but instead I have betrayed him!"

He began to clear away the adornments, and as he cried in repentance, his tears washed away the dirt on his teacher's grave.

The people heard his cries and gathered around him, saying, "Why are you crying? We know a true teacher would have a simple grave, and we can finally see the name of your teacher in clarity now. Indeed, he was a true teacher and a great man."

The man replied, "I was not his student until now."

The people asked, "How can that be?"

He said, "I was following myself. I shaped my teacher's image on my own desires. I did not see what I had done, and the man I presented was one that did not exist."

The people marveled at his insight. "Perhaps we have done the same?" they asked themselves.

After that day, each went and sought to find the truth about their own teacher. After some time had passed, they all came together and saw that each one's teacher taught the same wisdom, yet in different languages, using different idioms, and developing different traditions based on their own cultural symbols.

An Active Relationship

Long ago, I prayed to know God's mercy. A short while after my prayer, I met a man who told me, "I love and want to know God, but I struggle with laziness."

I helped him off his feet, got him food and paid for a hotel room for the man.

He asked, "Why are you being so kind to me? Is it for God's reward?"

I said, "Because you let me be merciful, you are my reward."

He didn't understand, so I explained, "You prayed to God, and the mercy you looked for came through me. I prayed to God and realized that to feel mercy, it must come through helping you, because when you are merciful to others, you bring mercy to yourself."

The man's eyes opened, and he said, "So if God is known through Action, then to know Him, I must be active myself!"

And from that very moment onward, the man was lazy no more.

Painful Recitation

My students asked me, "How can we deal with an addiction to reliving painful memories?"

I told them a story:

I once knew a man who was addicted to reliving his pain.

I told him, "Your pain says to you, 'Give me your energy and time, and I will listen to your moments of sadness.' And you stay because you feel this pain is the only one that values and listens to you."

I held the man's shoulders and said to him, "Now, give me your time and energy, and I will remind you of moments of happiness."

Some time passed as the man filled his days with making himself remember moments of happiness, and eventually, he fully recovered.

So, I said to him then, "Look back at your pain."

He looked and saw no one there except a mirror and a book.

"I'm confused," he said.

I told him, "The mirror is because the pain was not a person. It was you talking to yourself, reading from this book of painful memories."

He replied, "Then let us burn this book!"

I said, "No, take the book, and go and save others with the lessons found within it."

He laughed. "What good will it do?"

I said, "My book gave me the wisdom to save you."

Parents

A person came to me and asked, "I keep having dreams of my mother asking why I spit on her. But I love my mother. I don't understand!"

I replied, "You have a slightly heightened awareness, which allows this message to come to you in your dreams. Now you must stop mistreating women, and this dream will stop coming."

He asked, "Why would my treatment of women bring a dream about my mother?"

I replied, "Because dreams are symbols, and every woman *is* your mother."

I then turned to my students and said: "Tell he who disrespects women that he has forgotten his mother, and tell she who disrespects men that she has forgotten her father. May they one day learn to remember them, so that they may also remember God."

My students looked confused. "But these people know God already."

I replied, "Can a person who has forgotten their legs know how to walk? Can a person who has forgotten their mouth know how to speak?

"In the same way, if someone no longer knows their parents who raised them in the physical world, how can they truly know God, who created them in the spiritual one?"

"If any of you believes in, but acts contrary to my teachings, you have forgotten me as well."

Partnership

One of my students came to me and said, "Teacher, I know you told me to be patient in waiting for my significant other, but help me understand how to be. I see men who have whatever woman they wish for."

I sat him down and conveyed a parable:

> *There were once two brothers named Sareeh and Sabr with the same amount of wealth. Sareeh would hire servants from among the poor and dispose of them at his will.*
>
> *The people honored him as someone great, saying, "How attractive is the strength of Sareeh? He has servants come and go at his will!"*
>
> *His brother Sabr, however, stayed alone, holding his wealth, searching for the right partner to do business with for the long term.*

But people in the community mocked Sabr, saying, "What is wrong with you? Your life is wasting away. Just be like Sareeh and hire servants already!"

After much time had passed, the right partner came and joined Sabr. He and his partner were overjoyed and successful in all of their doings.

Sareeh came to him afterwards with a sad look, saying, "I have nothing left of wealth except for the last servant I hired."

Sabr said to him, "But I thought the last one you were with was your partner."

Sareeh shook his head saying, "That is what I told the people, but it isn't true. This is just all I could get with whatever value I still had left with me to convey. You have done rightly, Sabr, whereas I, Sareeh, was wrong."

My student understood. He stood up with strength and a look of happiness. "I want to be like Sabr!"

I smiled. "If you endure, then Sabr is within you, but if you are too hasty, then Sareeh is within you, and you will become what you do. Always remember that."

Patience

Patience while working towards a goal is like sitting on an empty train with no one to talk to except God, and at every stop, the people call you from outside to come join them, but you respond, "As much as I desire to join you, I cannot leave this train, for I have not yet reached my destination."

My students asked, "What about those who leave the train before their destination?"

I replied, "Their tickets are kept in a special place as evidence against them if they complain of never arriving, and it will be said, 'We sent our train conductors to help take you to your destination, but they came back to us saying, the passenger you ordered us to take has left; this here is their ticket."

Suppress Hatred

I told my students, "To entertain hatred is to accept its terms, to accept its terms is to respond with the same, and to respond with the same is to add fire to a flame that consumes both the one who kindled it and those who add to it."

My students asked, "Then what should we do to suppress hatred?"

I replied, "Find what is good in a person and entertain it. When you entertain the good, you invite the other person to accept its terms by responding with the same. To respond with the same is to add water to a flowing stream that cools both you and the person whose good deeds you brought to light. As it flows and cools, it extinguishes the fire of hate."

My students asked, "How does it cool both you and the other person at the same time?"

I replied, "Because when you constantly dig for the good people do, like digging for water, you unearth the waters of love, and people in turn will likely become inspired to bring up your goodness as well. Thus, they have accepted your invitation to respond with love."

My students asked, "And what if they don't accept the invitation?"

I replied, "Leave a person with nothing but invitations to hear the good of themselves, no matter how small, for showering a person with recognition for their accomplishments washes away their hate. And what greater suppressant to hate is there but Love?"

Perfect Imperfection

"Strive to be perfect in your imperfection," I taught my students.

My students asked, "How can someone strive for perfection while knowing they are imperfect?"

I smiled and reached into my pocket for the key to my house. I took it out and showed it to them. "Tell me, this key without its lock, is it perfect?"

They replied, "No; by itself it is incomplete."

I continued, "And if this key is finally joined with its lock but has lost its unique ridges, is it perfect?"

They replied, "Of course not, because its unique ridges were made for that lock. The key won't open the door without them."

"Exactly. Each of us is just like the key, which is imperfect in and of itself, but if you strive to maintain that which is unique about you, then the doors that were destined for you will open when the time comes."

I paused, reflecting on this, and then continued, "How many a door is never opened because people blindly sought to become misaligned with their souls, before they ever got the chance to find the doors that could only be opened by them?"

الله موجود

Prayer

A man ran up to me and said, "You fool! You teach that God is beyond human, and yet I hear you follow a human ritual to praise God? Your movements are no different from pagans before their idols!"

I replied, "Perhaps you are right. Advise me on what I should do."

Shocked, he said, "God is not in any one place! Pray wherever you want!"

I said, "You're right, but what if a place is unclean? I would feel disrespectful to pray there."

He said, "You should find a clean place to help concentrate better, but nothing more."

"You're right, but what if I am unclean? I wouldn't feel good while praying."

He said, "You should clean yourself before praying, but nothing more."

"You're right, but I don't feel humble standing straight when I first praise God."

He said, "You should lower your head while praying, but nothing more."

"You're right, but afterwards, I begin to feel even more humbled."

He said, "Then you should bend down and praise him when you feel that way, but nothing more."

"You're right, but after standing up again, I feel regret."

He said, "Then you should prostrate yourself in the humblest position, but nothing more."

"You're right, but when I sit up, I regret it."

He said, "Then you should go back down then, but nothing more."

"You're right, and when I get back up, I feel thankful."

He replied, "So you should then give thanks."

"You are right."

I noticed he had tears in his eyes after this. He looked at me with understanding. "No, you are right. I realize now that although God is beyond human, we are not."

And since that day, I never saw a man appreciate daily prayers as much as he did.

One of my students, overhearing all of this, asked, "We notice that you pray more intensely during times of ease, but not as much during times of discomfort. Why is that?"

I told him, "The connection God has with one who is broken from this world is magnified more than the one who is at ease with it. Therefore, I pray intensely at times of ease and say, 'It is only by your infinite mercy that my prayer will be accepted like those made in times of hardship.'

"I meditate on this until I break myself from the world again."

The Sweetness of Faith

I told my students, "You have heard the saying, 'The sweetness of faith is in good character.'"

My students asked, "What of those who don't believe in God but truly have good character?"

I told them, "Good character, for many, comes from their upbringing. They tie part of their identity to the morals and ethics taught to them by those who believe in God, and they consider the forsaking of those principles as a betrayal of self.

"But because God was made distant, unknowable, and contradictory by the arrogance, ignorance, and behavior of most religious folk, they subconsciously perceived a separation between those morals and ethics, and the God itself. Because of this, they could abandon God easily, while still keeping their morals and ethics.

"Some others, on the other hand, have an intuitive understanding of why things are good or bad, right or wrong, because of a heightened ethical awareness greater than that of those who have not developed such an understanding.

"But without belief in God, one must admit there is ultimately no source, and no real standard by which to measure these morals and ethics. Therefore, these people carry the sweetness of faith but refuse to label it as such."

My students then asked, "What about those who do believe, but say there is no reason for having religion?"

I asked them, "What are the elements of true religion? God as the foundation, the philosophy that comes with it, and a variable set of traditions that cleanse, maintain and reinvigorate the people who adhere to it.

"Those with good character, non-believers and believers alike, would be able to ground and preserve themselves by accepting and adhering to a true religion. For the world is filled with bitterness, and many who started off with the sweetness of faith have become bitter along the way."

Ready for War

A man came to me and asked, "I heard that you and your students are preparing for a war in which your weapons and armor are the same. What kind of war is this?"

I smiled and said, "The war I prepare my students for is a spiritual one. Our weapons and armor are our words, actions and integrity. But one cannot properly wield these weapons without gaining the upper hand over the war within themselves.

"Most people are anxious to battle. Untrained as they are, they pick up the weapons of words and actions to attack, but they hurt *themselves* more than they hurt their perceived enemy.

"You will see many cry out: 'Look, I am bleeding with anger from the attack of my enemy!'

"But it's because their souls still have self-inflicted internal wounds from the Ego that the enemy's attack even injures them. Blind to this, it increases their frustration, and they attack even more without knowing to heal first. This is the majority of people."

Amazed, the man asked, "May you give me examples of what principles you teach in your class about this?"

I replied, "I informed my students that no one's grip is firmer than those who truly understand that they own nothing in this world.

"My students then asked me, 'If not the things they own, then what are these people holding on to better than anyone else?'

"I told my students, 'The people who understand they own nothing in this world are able to hold onto *themselves.*'

"When attacked, know that smaller enemies can be destroyed simply with silence and a smile, for the game that is not entertained is dead without its opposing player, and the victors are recognized by their contentment.

"Those who favor insult and brazenness will ally with those who are like-minded. Those who favor respect and composure will ally with those who are like-minded. So be patient; the soldiers needed for the cause of the just will come without a rally cry. And those are the purest of recruits.

"Also, for any answers you wish to deliver when going into battle, you must maintain composure in giving them. Just as one who shivers when shooting an arrow will miss the target relative to the intensity of their shaking, so too will you give a less accurate answer relative to your loss of composure.

"Also be aware, Satan is not the one you point the finger at, but many times he is the one who tells you to point. Reflect on this before you approach any enemy, to first rule out the one who may lie within. Know that Satan will aim for you to fail, yet with every test you pass, he contributes to the credit needed to earn your success with God, and to the experience needed to heal the world.

"When you grasp this reality, you will look at your enemies with a smile, thinking, 'Come, insult and attack me! How can I not love my enemies? They provide the spiritual labor for my earnings.'

"And continue to smile, for there is no fear engaged that does not add to your strength.

"Always give praise to the righteous among a people at the same time that you criticize their wicked. This prevents conflation of the two and inspires those on the borderline towards peace and good deeds, without blocking their way with negative emotion.

"Also know that those who mention what is true as well as what is false in both sides of an argument bring Satan much distress, since doing so closes his avenues and nullifies the whispers of his minions into the hearts of men.

"If you wonder how to know if you're impartial in talks between one group and another, know that the one who is impartial is considered a traitor to a third in both groups, considered confused by another third in both groups, and considered honest among the last third in both groups.

"These values may fluctuate, but you will always find them among a people. Until the day when the last third becomes the whole, you must stay firm when insulted and never label an entire group. Instead, persevere and say, 'For the sake of the righteous among them…for the sake of the righteous among them.'

"One who labels a community by the worst of their members invites the same to be done for their own. And since the logic of a conversation is set by the initial speaker, all who join that conversation are compelled to do the same. You will find many of them saying they are staunch defenders of their community in this world, but they will be charged with the crime of destroying their community in the afterlife.

"Understand there are dead soldiers from both sides of war that will become best friends waiting to confront their leaders on the day of judgement.

"Do not be intimidated by those who are already ahead of you in knowledge and use this as a weapon against you. Focus on understanding wisdom first, which takes precedence over knowledge, for one can spew many words of knowledge, as an untrained marksman fires many bullets, hitting everything but the target.

"Whereas, one who knows the purpose of a gun, how it is supposed to be aimed and handled, can hit the target in a single shot, using just one bullet.

"Be brave, but drink moderately from the cup of self-worth, just enough to prevent anyone from making you feel inadequate, but not enough to cause you to become drunk, thinking yourself to be God.

"When injured, be aware that spirituality is used by the escapist like alcohol to run away in a world of self-righteous delusion, whereas the realist uses it to cauterize their wounds, gritting their teeth in repentance and humility.

"I will continue to teach you the ways to see into the soul of the enemy, to reveal their innermost fears so that they fall in front of you, regardless of their physical strength or affluence.

"My students had asked me, 'What about those who find and learn these ways only to become our enemy?'

"I told them, 'Those who fear you on account of your knowledge of God will fight and lose, or they will seek to know God. If they know God, they will fear Him, and those who fear God will never be a true enemy to one who does the same.'

"My students then asked, 'Of all good works, what should we place our general focus on?'

"I told them, 'Out of all the evils in the world, Satan loves most when families are torn apart. Come then, let us do the opposite.'"

Religiously Blind

I told my students, "For every religious idea you learn, become that much more conscious of the line between self-improvement and self-righteousness. For the value of remaining humble is larger the more knowledgeable you become, and the sin of pride greater, with a blindness few recover from."

My students asked, "May you explain this blindness more?"

I told them of a vision I once had: "I saw two people walking, holding the same set of tools. One was quietly using the tools to fix some loosened parts in their body. I noticed that shortly after correcting those parts, they would always become loose again, and they would quietly tighten once more.

"The other person was showing off their tools to the people around them, and every time they would brag with even the slightest nonverbal gesture, not only would their parts become loose, but their tools would become blunted, and they were unaware that they were no longer able to correct their loosened parts."

My students asked, "What does the vision mean?"

I replied, "The first person symbolizes those who use religious traditions properly to continuously correct and keep themselves in check.

"The second person symbolizes those who use religion improperly to boost their own egos. The traditions become ineffective and blind them to their own flaws."

Rewards from the Unseen

My students asked, "Teacher, why is it that some people receive divine help immediately when they call out, while some do not?"

I replied, "There are many reasons."

They implored, "Give us one reason that people are not aware of."

I told them, "When a person helps others in order to impress people and earn recognition, but never helps in private, that person has recorded with the Angels this statement of belief: 'Help should come from those who are seen; let recognition and praise be the reward for sacrifice.'

"Therefore, when they ask God for help, their rewards are spent, their belief is held as a wall against them, and there is a delay.

"Whereas, when a person constantly helps others in secret without looking for recognition, that person has recorded with the Angels this statement of belief, 'Help should come from the unseen; without receiving praise or recognition, let the reward for the sacrifice be with God.'

"Therefore, when they ask God for help, their rewards are remembered, their belief is an open bridge before them, and help comes quickly."

Significance

A man came to me in awe, saying, "I wish I could be as important as you and your students. I only work at a small food stand. My mind doesn't get big words or computers, and I just seem to always have great success with the small things I understand. I know I have to accept things the way they are."

I welled up with tears and told the man a story:

Many years ago, there was a man called Saghir, who owned a small bread stand. The only space he was given in the crowded marketplace was by the cliff-side at the edge of the city, but he went to work every day selling bread with a smile.

One day, he saw a boy with ragged clothes looking depressed and walking by slowly. The upper class were pushing the boy out of the way, and some of the sellers were yelling at the boy to move out of the street.

Saghir called the boy over to him and asked him about his day and his well-being, and gave him the same respect he would give any person he spoke to. After a short time, the boy began to smile and feel good again. He thanked the man for the conversation, and then left.

Many years went by, and life began to get better for those living in the city, because a new ruler had ordered many decrees to help the welfare of the citizens.

One day, the marketplace was buzzing with news. Saghir asked what was going on, and the rumors were that the new ruler had said the most important person they would ever meet lived in this city! They were all wondering who it was. As soon as they finished speaking, a royal delegation came into the marketplace. The king came out with his guards, and people gathered around as he was going from store to store, looking at all the people's faces. Everyone was confused.

Finally, the king saw Saghir and walked up to him. Staring, he began to tear up. The king asked Saghir, "Do you recognize me?"

Saghir responded, "You are the King."

The king smiled and said, "Many years ago, when I was a boy, I ran away from the palace and disguised myself. I was walking to the cliff-side where no one cared to look, and I was planning to throw myself off to prove how cruel and depressing life was with the royal family. But you called me over and spoke to me like a real person with decency and respect, and you showed me that there are still good people in this world."

The king then raised Saghir's hand and turned to the people and said, "It is because of the one you call Saghir, that I made the decrees that brought your life comfort when I

became King!"

The people cheered and said, "We made a mistake when

we judged you, Saghir, for you turned out to be the most

important."

After hearing this story, the man smiled and went into deep thought.

I told him, "Most people are not as open as the king to come back and tell you how one conversation with them influenced a decision they made which changed their lives for good, and how it ripples through the world. "Just know that on the day of judgement, we will find that many we thought important are indeed not so, and many who we thought insignificant, are those who helped change the course of humanity."

From that day forward, I never saw a man so joyous to speak to customers at his job like he was.

Taubah [Return Back]

There was a man who was highly respected and a leader of his people. The people cried to him, saying, "The outsiders call us murderers and liars; they blame us all for the actions of a few! Pray to God with us that this collective judgement ends!"

The man agreed and prayed diligently with his people. After some time, an Angel came to him in a dream. In the dream, the man cried with joy and said to the Angel, "Praise God! Has our prayer been accepted?"

The Angel replied, "You have not truly prayed, but we have heard your despair, and God sent me to help your people, yet your people told God to send me back."

The man then awoke, in a state of shock. He went to his people and said, "What have you done? An Angel came to me and said you've told God not to deliver us!"

The people said, "Never! Why would we stop our own salvation?"

The leader was confused and said, "I will pray again and see if God allows the Angel to return to me."

After many days, the Angel returned in his dream. The man cried to him, asking "Please tell me how is it that my people have told God to send you back?"

The Angel replied, "When you and your people ask for God's mercy, he sends me immediately, but when your people do a certain type of injustice, God, in his justice, calls me back, saying, 'They have said otherwise; return back.'"

The man was bewildered by this. "What is our injustice?"

The Angel replied, "To earn your salvation, you must come to know your injustice on your own, not be told by me."

Afterwards, the man awoke. In solemn tears, he went to his people and told them of what the Angel said. For the first time, instead of just asking God again, they sat and reflected on the matter.

Someone said, "We're asking to change how others view us, but how do our people view others?"

Another man shouted, "Most are murderers and liars! We've heard what they do!"

Another man said, "Not all of them."

Another chimed in, "This is our injustice! We ask to be seen rightfully, but then we judge others in the same way they judge us!"

Another man asked, "Didn't they start it?"

One said, "It's irrelevant now who started it, what is relevant now is who ends it!"

They all prayed together and made a public declaration distinguishing their harsh judgments for all other groups that they once labeled only one way.

That same night, the Angel appeared in the leader's dream, smiling, and said, "You have finally prayed to God in justice and removed the barriers."

The leader said, "Yes, we prayed after we realized our injustice."

The Angel said, "No, your prayer started the moment you began to trace back your mistakes. I will now do what I am designed for, and see to it that Satan does not cause you to go back on your words, or God in justice will immediately cause me to go back on mine."

Teacher and Student

"Do not listen to me alone. Seek those who draw from the same source from all nations so that you may always understand the difference between the source and the many constructs in which it can be given," I instructed my students.

My students asked, "But Teacher, there are many who claim to understand divine knowledge. How should we know who to listen to?"

I told them, "To the wicked, that knowledge is simply a mask from which arrogance and ill-intended sarcasm spill from the eyes and mouth.

"Whereas, the faces of those who have taken the time to understand divine knowledge are radiant, with humility and sincere encouragement flowing from their eyes and lips. I will teach you additional methods for determination, and for each the reasoning behind it."

I added, "I want you to know that I am both the teacher and the student of that which inspires me."

My students asked, "When are you the teacher, and when are you the student?"

I said, "When I am inspired, I have a brief opportunity to pull from the spiritual wellspring that existed before the creation of the physical world. I am the teacher when I give you that water to drink in a cup that you can understand, and I am the student when I myself become thirsty and seek to drink from that well."

That Which Purifies

My students asked, "Why are there some people who feel pain upon hearing the truth, and some who do not?"

I replied, "If one of you having a stomach infection drinks a bitter tea made of herbs, what will you feel?"

They said, "Pain and discomfort, after which the infection will leave."

So, I asked, "And if one having no infection drinks the same?"

One replied, "They will feel no pain, and it will prevent an infection from coming in the first place."

Smiling, I said, "So it is with the truth, which is bitter to the taste, removing the infection of illusions and falsehoods painfully. And afterwards it is a maintenance to prevent a return infection. After a time, you will find a sweetness in it that is beyond the senses."

The Birth of Sects

My students asked, "When will we begin to understand the truth?"

I replied, "You will begin to understand the truth when you love the scholars' unwritten desire to find it, more than you love their written shortcomings in grasping it.

"Know that most scholars write with the drive and vision to bring light to part of an idea that was ignored or neglected, but most of the followers of each scholar misunderstand this as a negation of the idea's other parts.

"When these followers hide or ignore part of a whole truth, it creates an imbalance. When the imbalance goes unchecked for too long, God then takes that part of the truth, gives it to another scholar, and strengthens their cause to rally people behind this ignored part of the truth, as a constant reminder of the sin of the former people.

"But without the previous parts, the new scholar's cause is also incomplete. Then Satan seduces the followers of that scholar to ignore another part of the truth, so then another split occurs.

"This continues over the years, with each sect remaining a thorn in each other's side until a complete truth is presented again.

"A leader from each community is presented this truth at least once in their life, but the temptation for self-honor and the sport of competition is stronger than the calm of reconciliation, and again the generation fails.

"This will continue until the thorns are too great to bear, until the heat is too strong, until all feel the sting no matter how far, and how seemingly disconnected."

The Broken House

My students asked, "How is it that children today despise religion?"

I answered them with a parable:

> *There was once a house with many rooms. The owner of the*
> *house gave each one of his children a room and told each*
> *one, "You will be given a window where light will come in,*
> *but be careful, from that same window, termites may come*
> *in. Don't be fooled, even though they come through the*
> *same window, they have no light in them. Make sure to*
> *exterminate them as soon as you see them."*
>
> *Each child agreed.*
>
> *Every day, light came in to each room, and every child was*
> *overjoyed, but each day a few termites would also come in.*

However, the children said, "These are so much fewer than we thought, what harm can they do? Perhaps we will deal with them another day."

So, they ignored them.

As time passed, each room decayed in different ways, and each child would criticize the other, saying, "Look at your room! It is from your room that the problems come!"

Each child was of course guilty, but because of their egos, each ignored his and her own room even more. In this way, the house became run down, with the children of each succeeding generation less willing to live in any of the rooms.

Looking at the house, they thought to themselves, "How can it be that God created something this broken and ragged?"

The Commander

"A true monotheist is so valuable, that a whole nation can be saved by one," I told my students.

They said, "Please explain to us how."

I replied, "There was once a commander who controlled a large group of people. And although he was the commander of all the people, there was one who remained beyond his control.

"One of the commander's closest advisors found out and asked him, 'How is it that you control these people and not this one?'

"The commander told him, 'I know the people's fears. Some are afraid of being poor, so I control the money. Some are afraid of loneliness, so I control the congregations. Some are afraid of criticism, so I control the culture. When you know people's fears, you can control them. But this one person only fears God. Therefore, I have no control over him, and he is always content.'

"The commander never sought to kill the one who feared only God, neither did he find cause to persecute him, because the man would praise the commander for whatever good works he did and be silent the rest of the time.

"This intrigued the commander, and he asked himself, 'How is it that this man has the strength to deny me? What gives him this strength?'

"As time passed, the commander began to learn of the man's teachings and character, and he came to find the man to be the only person he respected, as he very much admired the man's great strength.

"The commander began to emulate the man's ways and to teach the same, gradually pushing people towards the good.

"One day he asked the man, 'Tell me straight, how did you come to this level of strength?'

"The man began to cry tears of joy, which confused the commander. He asked the man what brought him such sudden joy.

"The man replied, 'I once was a commander like you. I controlled the people's fears until I realized I was the most afraid, and I had become a servant of everything I commanded, a slave to the image I had created. One day an Angel came to me and said, 'Fear God alone and you will truly be a commander of the people, even without ordering a word to them. And now it has come to pass that you have watched me and have begun following my actions. In doing so, you have guided the people that way as well. So, God has made me a commander again, without ordering a word to the people.'

"The commander broke into tears and said, 'On this day, I do also believe in God.'

"And it was so, that the entire nation was saved by the resilience of one man who truly feared God."

The First Commandment

My students asked me, "Why is it that some monotheists do not move forward in life and some idol worshippers do?"

I answered them, "Unfortunately, many monotheists still project all of their personal problems, fears, hopes and anger onto something in creation and thus become idolaters. They shape, amend and attach these issues onto something visible, in an attempt to bring comfort and reduce their anxiety.

"However, this only increases their anxiety, and they remain stagnant. And each time they mention that issue, they bow down to that idol saying, 'This has strength over me,' although they don't realize it.

"But those particular idol worshippers who you see move forward in life are only idol worshippers culturally. They don't live projecting all their personal problems, fears, hopes or anger onto the people or the gods they claim to believe in, even if they say they do when asked.

"They do not truly attach their issues onto anything visible, and thus they progress past them with hard work and focus.

"So, each time they bow to a physical idol for tradition, and yet they don't believe it can stop them from achieving, they are actually saying, 'I don't believe you have strength over me to stop me from moving forward,' and they know this in silence.

"There are those who religiously worship many gods, but they live as if they worship one. And then there are many who religiously worship one God, but they live as one who worships many."

The Harvest in the Fields

A group of people came to me and said, "Blessed are those who read the scripture and focus on it day and night. And cursed are those who are complacent in study. We stay away from them. They are doomed!"

I told them of a vision I had:

There was a man who sought after a fertile land owned by a King, saying, "I will spend my time on that which is truly important and which will also be in my later years."

I saw another man who did not think so, and he always spent his time with others.

At the end of their lives, they both stood before the King.

The first man was smiling proudly, saying to the second,

"Do you not regret wasting your time?"

The other man was fearful.

Yet, when the King arrived, he said, "You who spent time with others, step forward, and you who sought the field, step back."

They were both shocked.

The first man said, "How can this be? I spent my whole life tilling the King's field, reaping the harvests!"

The King said, "This whole time, you were so focused on being acclaimed in my eyes, that you did not stop to think why the field brings harvest. It was to give the harvest to others for them to eat, in addition to harvesting my fields.

"Yet your pride blinded you from that, and you did not share the harvest. Because of this, the uneaten wheat became putrid and stunk in the sight of people. And therefore, you caused them to hate my fields, and they stopped believing in me."

The second man spoke up: "But what have I done to earn your mercy, King? I am just a fool."

The King replied, "Yet what little you had from some fields, you gave to others. They ate from your food and were saved even for a short while. Therefore, you are higher in the King's eyes."

The people then asked, "Do you mean to say focusing on reading scripture is bad?"

I replied, "No, but I am here to remind you how easy it is to turn scripture into something for your own glory, which destroys its image, instead of using it for inspiring and helping others, which gives glory to God."

The Migrant Worker

My students and I were walking past a migrant who was cutting the grass of a rich man. The rich man and his friends were mocking and throwing branches at him.

I went to reprimand those men, and spoke to them in a language they could understand, saying, "Don't you know that what you put out is what is returned to you, and what also may fall on your children's generation as a curse to undo?"

They laughed in disbelief.

I then went to the migrant worker and said, "I am here to give you good news."

He looked at me with an odd expression.

I continued, "Despite being wrongfully abused by your bosses and citizens of the land, you and your fellow migrant workers still remain patient and trustworthy, and thus the mockery you endure pours like water over the seedlings of your good deeds.

"The time of your harvest will come, and those who abused you will be hungry, because they spent their water on you, so they will have none left for their own fields.

"In this way, you will become their boss, and they shall become the migrant workers.

"That time may not come in your lifetime, but it will come eventually. So, teach your children of eventual victory and to remember these words of caution: When you become the boss and those who ruled over you become like the migrant worker, do not abuse them. Do not cause the cycle to repeat itself back to you.

"Instead, break the pattern, so that the positions of bosses and migrant workers will not be influenced by the sin of mockery and wrongful abuse, but rather by hard work alone. This way, your future generations will avoid having to overcome God's punishment for those sins."

The Missing Lamp

I told my students, "One who has a valuable idea that they cannot explain in a practical way is like one who finds a lamp in a dark room but cannot light it.

"Imagine a group of people in a dark room. The people say, 'If only one of us had a lamp, we would be able to see our way around this room!'

"The one who has the lamp becomes angry and says, 'You fools! Don't you see I have the light?'

"But no one else can see because it is still dark, and they reply, 'Another claimant, another liar.'

"Then a fight breaks out, and the lamp becomes lost. Afterwards, the people continue to wander again aimlessly until someone bumps into and finds the lamp again, only to repeat the process."

My students asked, "Will the lamp ever become lit?"

I replied, "It will, but only when someone has the patience to find a way to light the lamp first before claiming they are the one who has it."

The One Who Tried

A man came to me in sadness, saying, "I feel as if I am in a state of constantly trying, trying for so many things that I haven't attained and don't know if I ever will."

I said to him, "A person is the sum total of what they believe, and every time they do something that stems from any one of their beliefs, they are simply reaffirming who they are.

"Don't think of yourself as being in a state of constantly 'trying,' since this will cause you to feel depressed and tired, attaining almost nothing.

"Rather, see yourself as constantly having the opportunity to testify to an aspect of your unique identity, and you will be happy and always full of energy, causing you to attain much more.

"And know in truth that among the greatest of life's attainments is being lowered into your grave knowing that the world knew exactly who you were and what you believed in, regardless of material gain or loss."

The man then said, "But I'm afraid if I make mistakes along the way…"

I stopped him, and said, "Don't be afraid, for each time you choose indecision out of fear, a part of you dies. A fearful person makes fewer mistakes, but it is as if they were dead. Whereas, a person who braves through their mistakes is alive and well."

After I said this, the man's eyes were opened. He hugged me and said, "I'm thankful and ready to tell the world who I am!"

To this day, I see him accomplishing many goals, leaving people in wonder and gossip.

The Right Interpretation

Two people came to me and said, "Tell us, which amongst us has the right interpretation of our scripture?"

I said, "Put the book in front of me that you both agree upon." They did so.

I said to one of them, "What is your interpretation?"

One man stepped forth, his eyes gleaming in fanatical joy, and said, "I see clearly it says God is only loving and caring. He does not care to punish, nor does He care about law--everything is permitted!"

I then asked the other one, "What is your interpretation?"

The man stepped forth with burning anger in his eyes, breathing heavily, and said, "I see clearly it says God is strict, and He tells you of his warnings and punishments! The law is strict! Anyone who disobeys will be punished!"

They looked at me, and demanded, "Now tell us which one of us has the right interpretation!"

I asked the first man, "Aren't you the one who allows all things in your household? Your children do whatever they please, and they mock you."

He was shocked. "How do you know this? You don't know me before today!"

Then I said to the other man, "And aren't you the one who banned all cultural celebrations in your household? Your wife says you go too far in disciplining your children, even for their slightest mistakes."

He was shocked as well. "Who gave you this information? You do not know me either!"

I replied, "Because neither of you have interpreted the scripture, you have instead interpreted yourselves."

They cried out, "How can it be then? We read the same words. How can we then know the true interpretation?"

I replied, "First, you must remove the interpretation of yourself from your nature. When you become clean, re-read the scripture. Then come see me again."

They agreed, and after much time had passed, they both came to me again.

This time, both were smiling with a calm and confident demeanor. They asked me, "May you tell us which has the right interpretation?"

I said to one of them, "Read your interpretation."

He replied, "I see that God loves and is forgiving, but He also punishes and gives us trials for growth. He teaches us laws but also exceptions."

The other one was shocked. "I have the same interpretation!"

I told them, "Aren't you both ones that have a balanced home, where you teach your children of faith, hard work, and both the good and the evil in this world?"

They both said, "Yes, we are, but haven't we again just interpreted ourselves?"

I smiled. "After you both conquered what was uniquely *wrong* in your different natures, you both shifted to a new frame of mind by which you correctly direct your thoughts and actions. Now, you are interpreting yourselves, and you have the *right* interpretation."

The Stain of Idolatry

I told my students, "There were many in the past who pulled from the Well of Wisdom and removed false gods from their midst. But the people among them still had the stain of idolatry in their hearts."

My students asked, "What is the stain of idolatry?"

I told them, "When a person puts what they can see over what they cannot see, they cannot separate the Wisdom itself from the person who pulled from it. And so, after each wise person dies, their people conflate the Wisdom along with the language with which it came to them, the customs into which it was encapsulated, and the personal struggles the wise person faced."

My students asked, "Didn't the wise ones warn their people of this?"

I replied, "They did, but the stain of idolatry hinders people from understanding their warnings, even when they read them daily.

"Intentionally and unintentionally, they change the meanings of words and ignore one part of the book while highlighting the other. And the different followers of each wise person fight against each other saying, 'This is the only way,' and many have died because of this lack of understanding."

I began to well up with tears. "Now tell me, can any of you stand by while watching your family members blindfolded reading a book and sitting idle? And when you come to take the blindfold off, they push you away, just as a parent wishes to wipe the dirt from the eyes of his son or daughter that they may see clearly, yet the child curses them and says, 'Do not touch me!'"

Then I stopped and could no longer speak coherently because I was drowning in emotion. My students sat there, frozen, staring at me.

Then they asked me again, "Teacher, how can we know if we have the stain of idolatry?"

I replied, "If you were to know of my sins, would it change your commitment to the principles and ideals I myself learned and taught to you?"

Some of my students instantly replied, "No!"

I then walked to those who had hesitated and said, "That moment you paused--that is the stain of idolatry."

The Unmarried Mind

The mischievous make pregnant an unmarried mind with the seed of hate. It kicks inside like a child struggling to come out, and the mischievous continue to incite negative emotion to help give birth to hatred.

When the action is born, the wicked come to take pictures, to give it fame, gossip and social value, which make the mischievous continue to be attractive to the unmarried mind.

I pray you miscarry any evil thought.

I pray you be divorced from the mischievous, and be married to the wisdom of the prophets.

May the seed of wisdom be in your mind.

May it be born into a good action.

May the righteous around you lift up and praise that good action like one who adores a beautiful child, so that you understand the value of your marriage.

And may it cause you to remain faithful and fruitful all the days of your life.

They Live and Don't Exist

A man came to me while I was teaching, and asked me, "How can you be an honest teacher? Some of the prophets you claim to believe in never existed. There is no evidence, so you must be following fairytales."

I smiled. "There are many people you see with your own two eyes whom the next generation will say did not exist."

He asked, "How is that possible?"

I replied, "It is those who stand for nothing, who follow all the trends blindly, who never speak against the majority, who bow to the money and fame of others. These are only remembered by their immediate family.

"And it is these people about whom nothing else exists after their passing, except printed documents in a few rooms, and images on computers. If destroyed like how things were destroyed in the past, no one would have anything to remember them by.

"But the prophets you mention made such an impact, that they affected the entire nation of people around them to remember, despite wars and destruction. It is they who existed more than anyone else."

The man paused for a few minutes in thought.

He then said, "I'm going to think about this. I hadn't considered this way of thinking before."

I then whispered a prayer.

The man asked, "What did you just whisper?"

I said, "I prayed that if you were living as a man who didn't exist, then may today be the day of your birth."

Those from Whom the Devils Run

My students asked, "We know that the Satan and his minions are sent upon some more and others less. How can we become those who are less harassed by the Satan?"

I answered with a story:

A man was thrown into jail and said, "Blessed is the Lord my God who punishes me as a father punishes his son, so that he may learn from his mistakes."

But the Satan said to him, "No! You are in jail for a crime you did not commit!"

The man replied, "Blessed is the Lord my God for refining me as a blacksmith refines steel to bear a greater purpose!"

But the Satan told the man, "No! You will die here!"

The man said, "Blessed is the Lord my God who has given me the opportunity to show others how a man with nothing can be content with the Master of everything."

The Satan countered, "No! No one will see you!"

The man replied, "Blessed is the Lord my God who has saved me from showing off to the people my dedication to God, and makes it so that my faith in Him stays for His sake alone."

The Satan screamed, "No!" and flung open the jail cell door to set the man free.

When the man asked the Satan why he did this, Satan replied, "When you first answered, your belief shook the angels on earth. The second time, it shook the angels in the sky. The third time, it shook the heavens. And the fourth time, it shook the throne of God Himself, and I saw the Shekinah [God's presence] descending in a way I have not seen since ages past. If I had not freed you, people would have seen it and believed."

After hearing this story, my students looked shocked.

I told them, "From this, understand that bad deeds are like a prison—when you begin to do the right thing, Satan's minions are disturbed, just like the body when it first begins to detox. It will be painful, and it will be a test for you. Satan's minions seek to discourage you, and they are allowed to do so, as part of your way of proving to yourself and God who you really are.

"But each time you continue to do good deeds when hardships or shortcomings occur in your life, you testify to God's presence even more, and it subsequently causes that presence to appear more in your life. Your life becomes full of miracles. The Satan begins to direct most of his minions away from you, in fear of the people noticing this and becoming inspired to do the same in their own lives."

Those in First Class

There was once a man who was afraid to attend my classes, since he was poor and feared being ridiculed by others.

One day, he stood outside of the first class. Looking in, he saw men and women who seemed familiar to him wearing simple clothing with no makeup.

He thought to himself, "Why do these people look so familiar? I do not see them in the later classes, but they must be poor like me."

Because he thought the people in the class were poor like him, he felt comfortable enough to come in.

He asked me, "I wish to accomplish much, but how can I when I have so little?"

I asked, "You have your life itself, do you not?"

He said, "Yes, but I have very little money."

I replied, "I teach the keys to material success, but only after I teach about the value of things immaterial. This is the primary focus for those in the first class."

He asked, "Why?"

I told him, "A person who doesn't understand what they already have is empty inside. They will seek physical earnings to fill that emptiness, but that which is physical can only become part of the physical body.

"Without understanding this, they continue to pursue material things only to become so burdened by their richness and fame that they eventually fall, realizing they have nothing inside to hold themselves up."

He was saddened, and said, "These rich and famous people are the ones I watch and revere."

Upon him saying this, many in the class began to weep.

He was confused. I took him aside and told him, "Those you watch and revere are the ones here in the first class."

Those Who Prepare Without a Sign

One of my students came to me in sadness and said, "I have no signs of progress in my life. Why should I continue to work hard as if there will be progress?"

I replied, "Don't grieve, for who are we to know which ingredients are needed first before the meal is prepared? And who are we to know the time it takes until it is ready? Who are we to doubt the maker of the feast?

"Instead, wash your hands when there is no food on the table. Sit upright in your chair and set your plate open in an empty room. Ready your utensils and prepare a smile, so that when the feast arrives, you are ready.

"When the feast arrives, others will ask, 'Why were you given such a large portion?'

"It will be said, 'Because they kept preparing with belief in the promise, and did not let silence disturb them.'"

The student asked, "What is the promise?"

I replied, "That while those who work with apparent signs receive their meals, those who work diligently and prepare in the sight of nothingness receive the largest. This is a fundamental law set by God from the start of creation, bound to His name."

Time for Prayer

"Teacher, we haven't seen you in a long while; we have so many questions to ask," my students said.

I replied, "Ask the one most pressing to you now."

They asked, "Which among the daily prayers are most beloved by God? Some among us read that it is the early morning prayer, while some find it is the late afternoon prayer, and yet others say it is the midnight prayer. We have sources that conflict with each other. How do we know which is true?"

I answered, "For some, it is the time just before dawn, but for those who are already up for another reason, it is not the same. For some, it is the peak hour of business during the early or late afternoon. But for those who are already free from work, it is not the same. For some, it is the evening or night prayer, but for those who have no obligation at that time, it is not the same.

"And for some, it is one of the precious hours of sleep during the middle of the night, but for those who work the night shift, it is not the same.

"So, know that the most beloved of prayers is the one that you do at a time where you have to sacrifice your devotion to a worldly thing that you were most attached to."

Then one of my students who was Muslim, like myself, asked me, "You told me once that if I turned my life around and started doing the right work, I would need to endure patiently, and that when Allah's time for me comes, I would achieve a better result than what I had imagined. What is it like?"

I replied, "It is like a person who realizes the time for Friday prayer late, but strives to come to the Masjid. When they arrive at the door, the Masjid is filled with those who came early. However, the person waits by the door patiently, and when the time for prayer comes, the people file in rank and space opens up.

"The person then walks in and continues to move up until they reach the place that was ordained for them, farther up than they expected. So, work hard, stand by the door, and do not turn away, for just as the call to prayer will come, so too will the call from Jannah come, and the Angels will open the doors for you."

True Love

A woman came to me and asked, "There are two men who have proposed to me. They both seem sincere in their love, so how do I know which to choose?"

I told her to bring them before me. When they came, I asked them, "Why do you love this woman?"

One of them said, "She is the most beautiful woman I have ever seen, she understands my job and values children and maintenance of the home, plus we have so much in common."

I then asked the other man, "Why do you love this woman?"

He paused for a minute and then said, "I do not know."

The other man laughed at him. I asked them to step out, and I turned to the woman and said, "Choose the second man."

She was shocked, and asked, "Why is it that you are so certain he is best for me?"

I replied, "The first man mentioned your beauty, but external beauty fades. He then mentioned his job, but this is based on the love he has for himself, not you. He then mentioned children and maintenance of the home. He mentioned the obvious, because he will not participate himself. Of all the things he finds in common *now,* those things will change with the course of life, and so will his love."

She was shocked even more. "And the second man?" she asked.

I said to her, "He does not know why he loves you, so your beauty can never fade. His job will always come second to you because his love for you will be his first. And he will want to participate with you in all matters of children and the home, because he is so concerned with his love for you that he didn't have to mention it."

She asked, "What about change?"

I said, "What he has is true love. It is not based on anything of this world; therefore, things of this world cannot make it change. Rather, his love for you will make all things common between you, no matter what happens in life."

Watchful Guards

My students asked, "What should we keep in mind about the circle of people we keep around us?"

I told them, "Align yourself with those of different perspectives who put their intellect over their emotions. They will be like watchful guards to you, warning you of enemies at the gates.

"And be wary of aligning yourself with only those who think as you do, since that is akin to surrounding yourself with mirrors. In your vanity, you become blind, and you will be a victim under constant attack.

"Do not take every emotional clash with your guards as a negative. First discern and reflect, because among friends, you will also clash with those who are truly close to your soul. Many people without understanding take a clash as a reason to distance from friends, and they continue to keep close those who they never clash with.

"But because of this, they end up distancing from the ones close to their soul, and instead they keep close those who are actually distant. Thus, these people remain in an unfulfilled state, while on the surface appearing to have the perfect circle of friends.

"Also, beware of having Anger itself as a guard, since it is like a person that stands by the gate of the mind and neither allows knowledge in nor out, without distorting knowledge with its grievances.

"Therefore, when you are angry, what you learn is tarnished, and what you are seeking to say is also tarnished; this drives your frustration even further.

"Be cautious of those always quick to disagree with you before you have explained yourself, but even more so of those always quick to agree with you in the same way. The most venomous snakes reveal themselves early on, by showing their impatient desire to be closer to you in order to inflict serious damage."

My students asked, "But what about those who always agree before an explanation out of sincere love?"

I replied, "That is not love, but rather obsession, and it itself is a poison that puts both individuals in danger, for this life and the next.

"Understand that genuine criticism is like the love of a close friend, and you will find that I am a friend of you all."

Who Bears the Burden

My students asked me, "What is our test in this world?"

I replied, "Know that all of your actions will come back to you, both good and bad. For most people, some of that good and bad come in this life, and some in the next. But if you make sincere repentance for your actions by humbling yourself in admittance, then those that are offenses to your own soul will be forgiven.

"However, for those actions where you hurt someone else and you do not seek forgiveness or were not aware, you will have to pay for them, either in this life or the next.

"Also know we are innocent of others' claims and actions, but we still suffer or benefit from proximity to, or connections with them. For does a child deserve to be born to parents who are irresponsible and cause them a deformity, instead of to parents who make health a focus to reduce the chances of disease?

"Does a child deserve to have parents who are wealthy or poor, prejudiced or wise?

"To be raised in a neighborhood which the people worked hard to make safe, or a place where crime and vice is the norm?

"But from birth to death, our reactions to those things which we did not sow, both the good and the bad, are also a part of the test, so persevere.

"Also know you are tested on your claims, the words of your own mouth that come with intent, for both benefit and harm. You will be tested on them whether you remember them or not, so persevere."

I then became silent, and my students understood that I had explained all of that which they could encounter of the test of this life.

They asked, "But Teacher, if all of what you described is part of the test of what happens to us from others' actions or our good and bad actions, what then is our personal test for ourselves?"

I replied, "Reflect and find what it is you feel in your soul that you are compelled to do. After finding it, discern whether that thing is considered ethically right. If it is, then your test is to see if you will do that thing. If it is not ethical, then your test is to avoid doing it.

"Through this, a soul can either increase in growth, or increase in resilience."

Wishing for Success

"Teacher, you have told us that we should hope for everyone to be successful in life, and in doing so, that we will be helped to reach our own success. But there are so many who do evil, as well as those who openly hate us, and some even wish to take our place. How can we understand this to be right?"

I replied, "The world is a machine, and all things brought into existence have a unique purpose. We, as humans, have the free will to fight against our purpose or take the time to find and embrace it.

"When one of us falls outside of their purpose, they malfunction, and the rest of the machine fails to work as efficiently. Those closest to the person feel the failure most, with the intensity decreasing as it ripples out towards all of creation like a wave. Those at a distance only experience it as small mishaps that they ignore or label as happenstance. However, we all feel these waves in ways we both can and cannot always understand.

"Those who hate or try to replace you only do so because they lack this understanding. So, to hope for them to 'truly' be successful is to hope for them to find their purpose and embrace it.

"After they find their purpose and embrace it, they will no longer have the desire to hate you, nor will they wish to replace you, because they will love their unique purpose and be content.

"This is why it is said that when the world finally reaches peace, hatred will die. All of humanity will understand their purpose, and all will embrace each other and wish for each other's success.

"Because to have people reach success, is to help yourself reach success."

I reflected for a moment, and then added, "Therefore, teach this prayer to the people: 'May that which you wish for yourself be that which you were already gifted to be responsible for.'"

A man then yelled out from across the room, "I hate people like you! Your belief is selfish, and you are doing it for the wrong reasons!"

With disappointment, I said to him, "Tell me, if I believe that part of my success is directly attributed to your own, then who is the 'self' that I am selfish for? Is it me or you?"

The man became even more infuriated and walked away.

I turned back to my students, who said, earnestly, "We truly hope for his success."

The Fields of the Righteous

A man asked me, "You respond to many, but I notice those who speak hate towards you are ignored. Why is that?"

I said to him, "You don't yet understand, but those who water the fields of the righteous the most are the ones who are most hateful. If I were to disturb them by reacting to their hate, I would only cause that water to pour back onto their field of hatred, thereby giving life to their crop of hate."

He asked me, "Then isn't it selfish to not admonish them?"

I said, "These fields are open to all. If they wanted to know the truth, they would take the time to look. The people who ask tell me they cannot see but wish to, whereas those filled with hate say they can already see but are blind, and the fields of the righteous do not belong to us. We are only caretakers for the owner."

He asked, "Who is the owner?"

I replied, "The owner is the Almighty, and as long as we remember this, we remain the caretakers of the fields of the righteous."

The Tree of Wisdom

One of my students came to me and said, "I have been pushing against the doors of wisdom to gain understanding like yours, but it is difficult."

I replied, "The reason you find it difficult is because you've been pushing on the doors when instead they open inwards. You do not go into Wisdom, rather Wisdom comes into you."

He asked, "But when will it enter?"

I replied, "When you unlock the doors."

He asked, "What are its locks?"

I replied, "Ego for the smaller doors."

He asked, "And for the larger ones?"

I replied, "Language, Tradition, Analogy and Metaphor."

He asked, "How is it that these can prevent greater Wisdom?"

I explained to him the parable of the Tree:

"True religion contains this greater Wisdom, but it comes like a fruit born from a special tree. The look of each fruit is different because they grow on different branches, some thousands of miles apart, and they sprout during different seasons with different skins.

"From its appearance, it looks as if the fruit of each branch is from a different tree, when indeed it is not. Most people only eat the skin of the fruit nearest to them, thinking they have eaten the whole of it. The skin is language, tradition, analogy, and metaphor. But the skin, eaten by itself, is bitter, and because of this, they make people around them feel bitter.

"They argue with those who have eaten other fruit from the same tree, because they were only ever aware of the difference in skin, not that which is common underneath. They think the skin of the fruit is the whole, and so they do not learn a greater Wisdom.

"Some other people eat the skin along with the sweet flesh of the fruit underneath. The sweet flesh is the meaning underneath the skin. By eating this, they become sweet and refreshing, making others around them feel the same. They notice other fruit that share the same sweetness, and they realize they are from the same tree as well. However, these people grow attached to knowing only their own fruit, and they do not learn a greater Wisdom.

"And then there are some, very few, who eat the entire fruit—the skin, the flesh, and the seed. Among those few are those who vomit the seed out right away from the pain, but then there are some who endure. Within those who endure, the seed slowly breaks down all preconceived notions, and it grows inside of them, sprouting throughout their entire being, bearing the greater Wisdom of the tree itself."

I looked away with tears in my eyes, and added, "These people in whom the seeds grow feel very alone, but yet they are compelled to teach others of why the tree exists, why there are different fruits, and why the skin of each fruit is the way it is."

The Cradle of Prophecy

My students asked me, "How does inspiration come to you?"

I told them, "Parables flow through me like an open cistern that lies before the clouds of inspiration. I do not know when it will rain, but when it does, I must be ready, for the handles and the spout of this cistern are my fingers and the pen, or my mouth and the sound of my voice.

"The climate of mankind is made hot by the Satan, so if I wait too long to pour, this open cistern's water of inspiration will be lost by evaporation back into the clouds, and I would need to wait until it rains again. I am obligated to give, for to give is my design, and my design is from 'The Designer.'

"May God grant that I collect and give this water all the days of my life, for the people thirst, and this water refreshes them."

My students asked, "Teacher, what is it that you've been teaching us?"

I answered, "About the one who is akin to the force between the middle of a cradled pendulum, which you cannot see, touch, smell, taste or hear, but that *facilitates the movement of* all that you can see, touch, smell, taste or hear.

"I have been teaching you about the one who is between the moment of a thought and its corresponding action.

"Between the moment of the two prostrations, and the two talks of the Friday prayer.

"Between the end of the rakat, the unit of prayer, and the rising to start anew.

"Between the end of the sixth day and the start of the first.

"Between the moment of a flower's readiness to bloom and the opening of its petals.

"Between the moment of the first expansion and the complete contraction of this Universe.

"Indeed, I have been teaching you about the One in the 'ו' between the two letters 'ה' and about the wisdom that comes with this understanding, to be able to know what will come from our thoughts, words, and actions."

My students asked, "What is this wisdom called?"

I smiled. "The cradle of prophecy."